T0284475

The Point of Distraction

The Point of Distraction

Will Eaves

TLS

TLS Books
An imprint of HarperCollins*Publishers*
1 London Bridge Street
London SE1 9GF

The-TLS.co.uk

HarperCollins*Publishers*
Macken House, 39/40 Mayor Street Upper
Dublin 1, D01 C9W8, Ireland

First published in Great Britain in 2024 by TLS Books

1

A catalogue record for this book is
available from the British Library

ISBN 978-0-00-843236-2

Typeset in Publico Text
Printed and bound in the UK using 100%
renewable electricity at CPI Group (UK) Ltd

This book contains FSC™ certified paper and other controlled
sources to ensure responsible forest management.

For more information visit: www.harpercollins.co.uk/green

For Andrew Frampton

The Point of Distraction

1.

I have been writing music again after years away from the stave and the keyboard. I'm not sure why. I suspect the answer has something to do with the feeling I often have that words push what I want to say away from me. Whereas music is like a radio broadcast from a distant galaxy: it comes to me in fragments, bits of code, none of it readily explicable. While it has grammar and organisation, it is not a language. It fills me with a sense of incredible relief. It begins with a sound in my head, often heard on waking, or else a snatch of melody or harmony grasped while I'm doing something else. The trick then is to catch some of it on the wing and transcribe it. You might think this is just like any kind of writing: have an idea, get it down on paper. But for some reason, in words the results are haunted by all the things I've misunderstood or failed to include, whereas the notes are patient and forgiving, however insistent the potential sound.

What is that sound? None of the stuff I write is ever likely to be played. I can't play much of it myself and other people are too busy. The phrases are hardly virtuoso, but I can see that they're tricky under the fingers, not ideal for pianists or cellists or oboists, and a lot of that awkwardness is a result of inexperience. And some of it is more deliberately unsounded because written music always occupies a resonant space between idea and realisation. It is an everyman's land to which the word 'theoretical' doesn't do justice. Meditation might be nearer the mark. Meditations are composed thought.

J. S. Bach's late incomplete masterpiece *The Art of Fugue* (1751, revised edition) is an essay in composed thought – fourteen brilliant 'theoretical' fugues and four canons, all in D minor, which can also be played (Angela Hewitt's version, for solo piano, is wonderful, as is Joanna MacGregor's on the same instrument). The composer's wrestling with abstraction comes over in the sound: each time someone plays it, we hear not just a performance but a new draft of something that has already been perfected in another realm. Frédéric Chopin's Preludes and Études, by contrast, are so much a part of the playable (though difficult) Romantic piano repertoire that it is easy to forget their provenance in a deep reverence for Bach.

Everything in Chopin is aimed at a real-world listener while at the same time being pregnant with almost unrealisable sophistication. Even an early pre-Paris piece, like the 'Waterfall' (Étude Op. 10, No. 1 in C Major, 1829), has that lovely balance between planned effect and unsounded homage. The bass, the land under the watery arpeggios, is a kind of hymn. The whole brief cascade could be a Bach chorale prelude.

We hear things in our inner world, and sound them in the outer one, where those things are different. My first job in journalism was as music editor of *What's On in London*, a listings magazine stuffed full of sauna ads, for which I interviewed Harrison Birtwistle. I wonder if he saw the piece. It was an article about his opera *Gawain* (1991), sandwiched between pages of telephone numbers offering a variety of happy endings in all keys. We chatted for an hour in a little room right at the top of the Royal Opera House. He was very tolerant. I said I'd been to see the English National Opera's *Peter Grimes* the week before, and he praised the production and performance extensively before admitting that he couldn't get on with the music. He said music that had been too well heard (like Benjamin Britten's) tended not to interest him as much as music in which the composer was still trying to hear something. Maybe he was making a version of the Bach/Chopin point about abstraction, and maybe not. I heard it as a truth about giving life to work, taking responsibility for one's creation without trying to control it. Michelangelo Antonioni, the film director, once said that it was important to him that his actors did not feel in control of a scene. He didn't say why, but I think it must have been for the same reason: artistically we needn't be in complete control because the reality is that we are not, anyway, and art is a part of reality.

My love of music, my sense of it as a radio broadcast from a remote galaxy, is connected with this matter of responsibility. When I write music, I'm absorbed by it. It almost abducts me. A compulsion is at work that has little to do with me personally. The music I hear seems to predate my awareness, or any claim to identity. As a child, I had a recurring dream in which I was set to drift through space in a capsule. I was completely alone, but comfortable and safe. I don't think it was just a uterine regression fantasy because the drift was active; I was on a trajectory. I was escaping something – my brother, probably – but also coming back to a state of silent contemplation, which felt exciting.

Galliards were popular Renaissance court dances in a spirited triple-time. The six beats to the bar/phrase accommodated five steps – the fifth beat had no step – and the whole thing went at a fair lick, with plenty of kicks and turns. Shakespeare mentions them a lot, so there's a loose literary connection to help me. (How often, like Sir Toby Belch, have I said to a man standing in a bush, 'I did think, by the excellent constitution of thy leg, it was formed under the star of a galliard'?) The dance is named for gaiety, so you had to be in shape to do it, and Queen Elizabeth purportedly danced six or seven every morning. It was often paired with a pavan, a statelier dance in simple time, and it is pavans rather than galliards that have survived musically, their influence traceable to the French overture, to the music of Maurice Ravel and Ralph Vaughan Williams, among others. But just because the galliard has fallen silent doesn't mean it can't be heard. Here is one now.

GALLIARD

for solo piano

GALLIARD

Grazioso ma precisamente ♩ = 85
p
3
l.h.
mf
r.h.
5
mp
7
tr
p leggiero
tr
mf

Galliard

9
mp
tr
p

11
pp
mp
mp
mf
tr
rit.

13
a tempo
p

15
tr
mf
poco grandioso
tr
f
p sub.
rit. e dim.
ppp sotto voce
pp
Ped.

2.

The question of what lasts is an engaging one. In Marc Shaiman's lovely lullaby 'The Place Where Lost Things Go', from that underrated film *Mary Poppins Returns* (2018), the magical nanny comforts a little boy who has lost his mother. She says that the nature of past love is mysterious, 'just behind the moon'; we can't know where it is, exactly, but it exerts an influence. It's the kind of good example you don't always remember or realise is at work in you. In that sense, it's like something you've mislaid, or indeed like Mary herself – weirdly inaccessible, beyond your control, but apt to turn up again.

Artistic forms – the shapes to which art inclines – express just this aptness. They keep coming back, and for two reasons. One is evolutionary. The shape that carries the music or the narrative or the architectural vision has proved optimally expressive over time. You cannot get around the fact that the arch, the story that funnels to a point, and the song or sonata or air-and-variations or blues that extend themselves by modification, are all shapes that recur, in every human age, because they're adaptable vessels. We rediscover aesthetically, as nature rediscovers functionally, what works best.

The second reason is more mysterious and relates to individual cases. Something appears to be lost that is not altogether lost, just biding its time, quietly. This might require a geological metaphor. Some human shapes vanish only to find their way back unexpectedly. Like creatures that have fallen into soft mud, been mineralised and returned as fossils, they reappear, frail yet obstinate, and more themselves than ever, unearthed by a wandering hand in an archive or a builder's spade. The weight of years lifts like mist. There they are: *Beowulf* (in the British Library's lightly burned Nowell Codex), the *Mary Rose* (in the saving Solent mud), the piano studies of Hélène de Montgeroult (printed but ignored), the letters and the notes you'd forgotten.

The evolution of an artistic form is a matter of repetition and staggered development, the verse epic (for example) slowly coming down to earth in vernacular prose as a novel while retaining the essential elements of quest and romance. But the reappearance of a specific, influential shape is often just ... staggering. Way back, a lovely object was abandoned. Someone died, inevitably; but the ice-age comb, carved from deer horn, or the gap-toothed piano in the corner, survived. And it might have been otherwise; the archivist and builder might have been less curious, busier, more preoccupied. The house's new owners didn't want a piano. You could have thrown out that box of correspondence. Once reclaimed, however, once opened, the fact of these things existing, and having existed for so long apart from you and your designs for living, makes itself felt. So much of our expressive culture harps on about the desire to create. Perhaps the extent to which beautiful things already exist – such riches, did we but see them! – is too little acknowledged. And what they express is a property of art for which there's no single term because it has to do with bringing things to life by disappearing oneself.

The moving Buddhist parable of the jewel in the cloak, from the Lotus Sutra, captures this precisely. A poor man visits a friend, gets drunk and falls asleep. His friend sews a priceless jewel into the hem of the poor man's cloak. When the man awakens, he goes on his way, searching, working, often begging, making do with little, meeting great hardship for many years. Eventually he meets his old friend, who points out to him the jewel. The poor man is overjoyed: he realises what it is that he has always possessed, the symbolic seed of enlightenment. But – and this is where my interpretation arguably parts company with Buddhist teaching – it is a realisation in two parts. For it is not just that he has overlooked the riches he already possesses, but that the revelation of riches depends, in a profound way, on the act of over-looking, the years of mistakenness.

You must be willing to let your artistic convictions, your chosen road, disappear.

It's a matter of getting out of the way. When I edit essays and articles, I am wary of the writers' declared aims (their emails to me usually describe a piece they've wanted to write, and not written) but more interested in what the pieces themselves need to be. In *The Leopard*, the twentieth-century Italian novel about the *risorgimento*, by Giuseppe Tomasi di Lampedusa, Prince Fabrizio finds refuge from society in a library. He 'felt at his ease there; it did not oppose his taking possession, for it was impersonal as are rooms little used'. It's a significant moment: Fabrizio is learning to relinquish his role as patriarch and father. Similarly, to further 'our' artistic interests, we must, like the parents of children, learn not to insist on identifying with them. It is for this reason that impersonality remains an important and haunting quality in the making of art, in which – though we may not be aware of it – we yearn for the absence of ourselves.

Such a yearning must be accepted for what it is: a spiritual feeling, a response to currents in the unconscious that carry our love of life, acknowledgement of pain and acceptance of mortality. On the surface, of course, we have declared aims and objectives. George

Orwell wrote, he said, because there was 'something [he] wanted to say'. The young Igor Stravinsky told Nikolai Rimsky-Korsakov that he wanted to be a composer. Clarity of purpose is important if we are trying not to kid ourselves or give in to orthodoxy. But that is just the surface. Beneath such declarations, there is what we discover as we begin any apprenticeship: that the work itself has surprisingly little to do with our conscious purposes. It seems instead to be about overcoming preconceptions, discovering unanticipated lines of argument, or submitting to discipline; finding that with our heart in something, however difficult it may be, we work selflessly, almost objectively.

In his memoir *Chroniques de ma vie* (1936), Stravinsky begins by describing his original determination to learn composition 'solely by my own efforts' with all his 'inherent aversion to dry study'. But what he thinks he wants isn't what he really wants – or isn't what the compositions want for themselves. Very quickly he comes to love 'dry' counterpoint, which he pursues under supervision and then on his own 'with more and more interest', hardly noticing that switch from supervision and conscious development to impersonal dedication and immersion. Instrumentalists will recognise this process of 'going under': the painstaking business of practice and learning that leads gradually to a loss of self-consciousness and a new kind of artistic awareness.

Not long ago, I found in my attic an almost sodden box of old papers, among which was a music manuscript for an organ solo called 'Carillon'. I recall the circumstances of its composition very well. I wrote it when I went to visit my friend and teacher Kevin Duggan on the Danish island of Ærø in the winter of 1991/2, travelling there from Norway, taking midwinter ferries from Oslo to Frederikshavn and from Rudkøbing to the port village of Marstal, where Kevin was organist. The organ in Marstal Kirke is a fine instrument built in 1973 by Frobenius & Sons; its modest specifications – two manuals, twenty stops including pedal – do not prepare you for its power and bright-edged versatility, a feature of all Frobenius instruments (there is a good example, in this country, at Robinson College, Cambridge). Everything from the reediest fantasias and toccatas of Jan Sweelinck and Bach to the grandest colorations of Olivier Messiaen sounds vital and fresh in Marstal Kirke, where, one whited-out December afternoon, Kevin played me Maurice Duruflé's Prélude et Fugue sur le nom d'Alain, Op. 7 (1942).

Duruflé threw out most of what he wrote, so we may be glad he kept this (though, as I see it, the throwing-out was a part of the finding). A magnificent and desolating piece, it was written to commemorate the young French composer Jehan Alain, who died in action at the beginning of the Second World War.

The fugue made a particularly strong impression on me. The main subject is a stepwise exploration of the D minor scale and triad that is half plainchant and half 'scissors tune' – the term song writers use for a theme that works by establishing the octave and then cutting down the interval bit by bit. (You can hear what this sounds like if you listen to 'Over the Rainbow'.) The heart of Duruflé's subject – what makes it so dramatic – is a step from D to E, two-thirds of the way through the five-bar phrase. The E forms a suspension that takes us over the bar line and hangs in space for a beat; you can feel as-yet-unsounded harmony moving beneath it, tensely waiting. The important thing to grasp is that the riches of the harmony already exist; the whole architecture of the fugue already exists; it is not being invented but discovered.

The first pieces I wrote at school were attempts at the kind of music to which I had been drawn by familiarity: little fugues, mostly, because I loved the unfurling nature of baroque counterpoint, where the final construction exceeds the sum of the parts. (This is even truer of a variational form like the passacaglia or chaconne, but we will return to those.) I also wrote suites for organ, because I was learning the instrument at my local church, and my sporty but enlightened comprehensive school had at last conceded I would never set the world of rugby on fire. My games afternoon might as well be spent practising, they thought, and I remain grateful to them. But 'Carillon', written miles away from home, after university, was the first thing that I got right – that I allowed to be itself and not a diagram of my efforts to write something fugal or French or plain weird.

Looking at it now, I can see that it makes a kind of statement about being free, or letting something else emerge, which embodies the paradox of effort and impersonality I still find appealing: I'd met my first boyfriend and was very happy. As I joined the human race, or so it seemed, the blockage of self temporarily dissolved. The whole piece, as its title suggests, is a peal of bells, with clusters of sound that unconsciously summon things I loved for themselves rather than things I'd previously wanted to emulate. The opening scissors motif has a kind of minimalist insistence at first, which is soon offset by a stepwise manoeuvre (Duruflé) in the left hand, like a fragment of a chorale or something from *Jaws*. Things get clamorous quite quickly – I remember playing Kevin 'Alphabet St.', with its interweaving lines and voices, and making the argument that Prince was a natural polyphonist – and the stepwise manoeuvre passes from hand to hand and to the pedals while the pealing clusters get louder and louder, with added mixtures (loud harmonics) and a variety of entries at different pitches if not in different keys. The tonality is flexible, but always comes back to C. The ending is what one of my friends calls a big-frock finish: both feet down on the pedal board, earplugs in, all the stops out.

When I got back to London, my boyfriend said he'd changed his mind about me, about us, and I felt the usual things: a blow to my pride, inadequacy, humiliation. I knew these things would pass, but I also wanted to hide. I knew that for all its intensity what I felt was ordinary, a kind of hard work, the beginning of a period of dry study. And that I'd have to go through it again in the future, maybe several times, in different ways. Wrapped up in this was the sick-making feeling that these emotions also mattered to me for artistic reasons. Humiliation is necessary to art and always there: from the outside you see only the ego's response, which is loud and compensatory. *I'm this. I'm that. I wanted to write a –. I wanted to be a –.* None of it very convincing. Much deeper, truer, runs the suspicion that shame – *how* could I have been so stupid/naive/wrong? – is a vital quality, because creation is externalisation and the urge to shed one skin and grow another that comes from being exposed is a crucial starting point.

'Never to be yourself and yet always – that is the problem,' as Virginia Woolf says. But right then, as a twenty-one-year-old, 'Carillon' and the writing of music – my first real love – were too painfully associated with that exposure, so I gathered up my papers and put them in a box. I couldn't see them for what they were. On their own, maybe, they had a chance of falling into the mud and being rediscovered later, having shaken me off.

CARILLON

for organ

This piece was written for the Marstal Church Organ, built by Frobenius & Sons, on the island of Ærø in Denmark.

Marstal Church Organ, Ærø, Denmark

Frobenius 1973/1995*

Main C-g‴	**Positive C-g‴**	**Pedal C-f′**
Principal 8′	Gedakt 8′	Subbas 16′
Rørfløjte 8′	Rørfløjte 4′	Principal 8′
Oktav 4′	Tværfløjte 2′	Nathorn 4′ *
Spidsfløjte 4′	Quint 1 ⅓′	Rørfløjte 2′ *
Oktav 2′	Dulcian 8′ *	Fagot 16′ *
Mixtur	Tremulant *	

Couplers: M-P, Pos-P, Pos-M.

Carillon

for organ

I	Main	Rørfløjte 8′ + Oktav 4′
II	Positive	Gedakt 8′ + Rørfløjte 4′ + Quint
Ped.		Principal 8′ + Pos-P

20
+ Subbas 16′
23
+ Oktav 2′
27
30
I
+ Mixtur
II/P

1991 / January 2nd, 2023

3.

Two years ago, I was passing a piano in a corridor; I sat down and obeyed the impulse to play a few notes, which turned out to be the first two bars of a piece called 'Curlicue'.

I was doing a teaching job and coming to the end of a commission to edit a book written, just about, by a senior politician. Ordinary paid work has always been a necessity, and my life has been spent mostly as a sub-editor and university teacher. Necessity has also been a source of inspiration. You cannot hang around waiting for lost things to jump out of boxes. Artistic inspiration may be an 'involuntary idea' (Freud) or a granting of permission in respect of unconscious gestures (Jung), but it's also bound up with the stuff you do to earn that permission. The unconscious is like a wary but curious animal: it comes to you because you have the food – the power of articulation – it needs, and it won't come if you stand there making kissing noises. Do something else. Look busy.

Hackwork never prevents better work happening. (It often turns out to *be* the better work: who doesn't prefer Erich Korngold's film scores, for *The Adventures of Robin Hood* and *The Sea Hawk*, to his art songs?) The danger, on the contrary, is that one stops paying attention to whatever it is one *is* doing and develops a fear of distraction. This neurosis has twin aspects. The first disparages routine: *I am always being distracted* by hackwork. The second refuses the gift of the unexpected: I am doing my better work and *I must not be distracted from it*. Behind both aspects is a presentiment of failure, a feeling of dissatisfaction with actual circumstances. I'm isolating this fear in respect of artistic aspirations, but of course it has a wider developmental resonance, as the British psychoanalyst D. W. Winnicott understood. What I have called fear of distraction, he calls 'a relationship [of the individual] to external reality which is one of compliance, the world and its details being recognized but only as something to be fitted in with'.

The problem for the artist is one of blind spots and stubbornness. Specifically, it is compliance with a mistaken conception of the task in hand. The twentieth-century philosopher Jacques Maritain talked famously about the habit of art – an appetite for making that requires skill and application – but neglected to add that this habit is variational rather than repetitive. It is a routine of work, not a method. Habit doesn't reveal one path or way to achieve an objective. In fact, it often seems to leave the objective untouched, like a satellite orbiting a planet, or someone enjoying a walk. There are many ways to the waterfall, and the varying route preserves for the artist a sense of surprise in the realisation of, say, a novel or a symphony, or an album, that carries over to its audience.

But routine and method are often confused, and then the results are zombies, things that totter about under a borrowed volition. Among literary people, especially, there is the dispiriting notion that, with a bit of graft, they can identify a popular template; that they can 'knock out' a thriller, because Elmore Leonard and Patricia Highsmith did it, so there must be a method, a trick. Fixed positions are adopted: *I wrote one book this way and now I will do it again. 'Story' is three acts, something called a turning point, and a cast of relatable characters.* Too bad if you thought characters should have priorities other than the reader's. Additionally, the belief that there is 'a way' to write a novel, or a piece of music, leads to a view of form that is anachronistic. You still hear critics saying things like: *Mozart expanded the possibilities of the sonata form.* Sadly or not, he didn't know of its existence. The musical journey from one melody to another – through different keys, tone colours and views back to a transformed conception of their origin – had no such name. It took place within older, fully absorbed conventions on the understanding that they, too, were apt to change: the theoretical principles were developed in retrospect. A model has to fit the music, not the other way around.

The need to believe in a set of rules or a method also has a more general connection to Winnicott's idea of delusion: *I need to be more this/that. My diet is killing me, but I love its rigour.* That way of thinking – and living – will run out on you, but it is attractive, or dating app profiles with manifesto-like criteria for meeting people wouldn't exist, and it is particularly tenacious when we encounter familiar difficulties – creative or otherwise.

Neuroscientists and psychologists call it the *Einstellung* or set effect. (*Einstellung* is German for 'attitude' and our idiomatic sense of that word, as a kind of stubbornness, is exactly right here.) It finds that a general tendency exists to favour known methods in problem-solving at the expense of alternatives, even when we think we're looking for them. If you have ever tried a key in a lock and discovered that, though there are other keys to be tried, you prefer to carry on jiggling the one that doesn't fit, then you have demonstrated this tendency. In 'The Mechanism of the Einstellung (Set) Effect: A pervasive source of cognitive bias' (*Current Directions in Psychological Science*, 2010), an experiment by Merim Bilalić et al., the phenomenon is studied in relation to chess players attempting 'smothered mate', where a mated King is trapped by his own pieces. Shown slightly different configurations of the chessboard, to which there are better solutions, the players – and these are good players – seem keen to stick with their first fixes. So we can be confident that clever brains are as susceptible to this effect as those that still think Brexit was about economic opportunity.

The *Einstellung* effect is also a good way of describing what can happen when an artistic approach stops producing results. For instance, it dawned on me, when I finished *Murmur*, a short novel about AI and suffering, that something was over – that I would not be writing that way again. (My usual routine, up to that point, had been to convince myself a book consisted of between ten and fifteen chapters of roughly 5,000 words each, through which I made my way from start to finish.) I'd felt the presence of the protagonist, a tortured scientist, in *Murmur* as I worked on it, and the experience unnerved me. As a follow-up, I considered a historical fiction about a road-building slave in Roman Britain and another one about silent cinema. Subconsciously I think I cleaved to the idea of a big task with parameters. Neither of the new books 'took'. The pre-literate and non-verbal themes perhaps indicated the real obstacle, which was one of compliance: the fixed-stare belief that I had to work in words to find more words.

It can be hard to accept the glimpse of 'something else'. It can feel like a summary judgement passed on months, or years, of effort (you've been cheating on yourself and only just found out). And though a glimpse of the productive unconscious is only ever a glimpse, it has the force of truth, as if one were to notice in passing a roadside drain and see lava bubbling up between the bars. This is not the way things should be, says the cool, solid world around you. No, says the lava: but it is now the way they are.

That reminder of the way things are (in the sense we have from geology or quantum physics that something very odd underpins our day-to-day reality) could be one way of thinking about creative insight more generally: that it is a counter-intuition aimed at refreshing our sense of what was there all along. A looking-away that turns out to be a looking-again. The distraction or digression – in my case the skein of notes on a rehearsal-room keyboard – feels strange only because of one's position in time. To begin with, it looks irrelevant, crazy, self-defeating. Later, it shows itself to have been necessary. Digressions are the maddening occasions when people break off from their story but come back to it having blurted out the truth. Perhaps what one is looking for artistically, then, is a mechanism that allows for a maximum of departure in the belief that all will come good, that the blurting can be corralled, turned to account. The poet Thom Gunn spoke of the 'trusting search' for a poem's identity, which puts it very well.

In music, one of the mechanisms that inspires this trust is – perhaps surprisingly – repetition. The conventional view of musical repetition, whether it be melodic or harmonic or rhythmic, is that it aids memorability: listeners struggle with unalleviated novelty to remember a song or a piece, even to understand it as music, and so they need recognisable elements to find their bearings. In fact, this is misleading, because the satisfying part of repetition – the point of it, indeed – is that it, too, is novel. Strict repetition cannot exist. A refrain or a ground (a repeated pattern in the bass) is never the same, even if the notes are identical, because music is a temporal art and to circle round a tune, play Scarlatti with repeats, sing 'Frère Jacques' or vamp with Stevie Wonder is to lift the repeating circle out of itself, like a coiled spring, so that it becomes a spiral.

An 'ostinato' (Italian for stubborn) is a musical figure that repeats in the same voice. It is supposed to repeat exactly (but see above) and it is familiar from all periods of classical music, every kind of drumming, modal jazz, funk and rock. If you like the clavinet riff in 'Superstition', you like ostinati. It can be monotonous if the composer is lazy. But it can also be liberating. Musical invention is the kite flown from the 'ground' up, one might say. The ostinato is a trippy device. It can be ritualistic (*The Rite of*

Spring) or sexual ('I Feel Love'), or both. And however daring the free variations worked on the motif or ground, those freedoms feel inherent, as if they belong somewhere.

Two of the stateliest forms of ostinato-based music in the baroque period were the passacaglia and chaconne, emerging in the seventeenth century and maturing in the eighteenth to become vocal or instrumental variations over a bass pattern (the passacaglia) or chordal progression (the chaconne). In both, the tension between constraint and freedom is maintained. Some version of a circle-of-fifths bassline or chromatic descent is often used as the ostinato, which ends with a cadence, whereupon another variation starts up immediately. Nicholas Britell's eighteenth-century influenced score for the TV show *Succession* is a good recent example.

Part of what makes these constructions so impressive is their mantra-like quality. As the ostinato pattern comes round again and again, it enters a raised dimension, lifted out of itself like a mountain whose summit we can't quite see. Our conception of the totality changes and becomes open-ended. The sense of the 'still possible' we have when we listen to baroque passacaglias or chaconnes – to Bach's 256-bar 'Chaconne' in the second partita for solo violin, for example, or Handel's 'Passacaille' at the end of his seventh keyboard suite, or Purcell's 'When I Am Laid in Earth' (*Dido and Aeneas*) –

derives from this patient deferral of the plain view. A little matter, the music says, is not always a little matter, and the end of something isn't the end of everything.

Because I'd dried up in words, I found myself looking again at that little phrase on the piano. It was a slow sarabande-like curling-about in the left hand, using a broken B chord followed by notes from the A minor and E minor triads. E minor, all in all, but not definitively: I couldn't see that being the key signature. Another phrase in the right hand, also bringing the melody back to E minor, made me think I'd come up with two themes, until I went on a bit, looking again at the phrase, repeating it, and found that the two themes were the same theme, split between the left and right hands. What I had was a small passacaglia, with the pattern shared out across the keyboard, between 'voices'.

Perhaps because I am a miniaturist by nature, I couldn't conceive of this little musical episode as anything other than a short piece. I often have a quick intuition of the overall shape of a story, and so when I looked back at the finished piece I wasn't surprised to see that the five-bar phrase had been subject to five variations, describing a kind of 5 × 5 square – like a decorated tile. But the open-endedness of bigger passacaglias made itself known in other ways, first by suggesting that 'Curlicue' could have another use as music for an audio adaptation I'd written a while ago – so words came in again by the back-door – and second, by suggesting another piece entirely.

Looking away from 'Curlicue' involved looking again at it – and especially the tied notes that were part of its curling motif. The second piece, 'Mote Turning', is a gentle examination of what happens when a tied note inside a chord transforms a melodic fragment, in this case one that describes the interval of a fourth. The answer is that a snippet of chromatic 'business' turns out to have consequences, both dreamlike and exploratory, although little new material is introduced after the first six beats. (I may also have been tapping memories of playing one of Domenico Scarlatti's most beautiful and economic slow sonatas, K8 in G minor, where the elaboration of a four-note cadential phrase has a similar interiority.) Both pieces seemed to want to slow down my wandering attention and to suggest a marriage between fragments, which is how many extended pieces of music – whether they be sonatas, suites, symphonies, song cycles or albums – come to be written, the separate bits and pieces gradually shedding their unrelatedness and revealing a shape.

TWO ORNAMENTS

for solo piano

TWO ORNAMENTS

1. Curlicue

Curlicue

November 1st, 2021

2. Mote Turning

Mote Turning

January 16th, 2022

4.

How does a piece of work come into focus? When do artists know that they have a poem or a book, or a song, or a sonata on their hands? The point of creative inception is a mystery: it can come from anywhere, at any time; it can be a starburst revelation or a creeping anxiety. In an interview with Murray Schafer, the British composer Michael Tippett said that he felt 'a need to give an image to an ineffable experience of my inner life'. At my lower level, I agree with him, in part because I'm reasonably sure Tippett, who had a sense of humour, didn't always trust 'ineffable experiences'.

But he was serious about finding an 'image', and here we encounter a peculiarity about artistic ideas of making. For although music is sonic and unfolds in time, both Mozart and Beethoven (and Schoenberg, who started out as a painter) spoke of apprehending work visually, in the first instance, and with remarkable completeness, before they'd written a note. Arguably – as Tippett goes on to suggest – they were conceiving and planning rather than seeing. We use phrases like 'artistic vision' in the knowledge that we are employing an analogy or metaphor to describe both the sudden nature of inspiration and the searching quality of hard work – distraction and compliance, in my terms – and yet the metaphor is so common as to make me wonder if it is a metaphor at all.

If we think of artistic envisioning as a kind of *navigation* through complex territory, then the metaphor acquires creaturely precision, with a few surprises along the way. What follows is a little eccentric, and probably personal to me, but it is based on the simple idea that physical 'seeing' is already a varied mode of apprehension.

How, in everyday life, do we know where we are? The answer is that our view of a landscape makes use of remembered abstract information – an internalised template or map of space – to tell us where objects are likely to be. Objects and landmarks matter, too, but the spatial map is important because it works in concert with active looking (the depth perception acquired by binocular vision, for instance) to reveal distance and help us orientate ourselves. This idea can be extended to other mammals, as an exercise in comparative psychology and with allowances for their variety of optical mechanisms. For a long time, too, it was thought that birds did something similar, matching object cues to spatial memory. But recent research ('Taking an Insect-inspired Approach to Bird Navigation', *Learning & Behaviour*, 2018, by David

J. Pritchard and Susan D. Healy) suggests that the avian world, or at least some of it, is closer to that of *insects*, where a map or remembered view is less important than what the animal sees when it's moving.

For example, when a bee flies sideways or in an arc around a flower, it is generating motion parallax – a depth-perception cue in which nearby objects move faster than objects further away – to identify its food source. Mapping still goes on, but at a dynamic level: location is revealed as much by motion round an object as by the object itself. Hummingbirds approaching a feeder have been seen to behave similarly.

The intriguing question is: do we? According to a famous account, from 1822, by the Darmstadt violinist Louis Schlösser, Beethoven described his process of planning a new piece in the following terms: 'I begin to elaborate the work in its breadth, its narrowness, its height and its depth ... It rises, it grows up, I hear and see the image in front of me from every angle, as if it had been cast ... [and] very often I work at several things at the same time.' In other words, it is the composer's mobile consideration of the 'work' – seeing it move, moving around it himself 'from every angle', like a bee or a hummingbird – that reveals its nature, not any kind of given appearance.

If the animal comparison seems extravagant, then it is worth remembering that humans use motion parallax, too; we just don't notice that we're using it. Cycle along the road, look to one side, and you'll see the pavement moving by in a blur, with the houses set back from the road passing more intelligibly. Such experience of relative motion in a turbulent world helps clarify depth, the three-dimensionality of the visual field and your sense of where you are in it. Perhaps 'artistic vision' works this way, too. Perhaps it *is* a part of physical seeing, in which the details of the work are not as important as the work's rising shape; where ancillary visual processes (parallax, peripheral awareness, looking away or looking sideways) matter more than locked-on focus, and where (maybe most important) an always-changing spatial cognition helps us to trust in the existence of the thing we haven't yet fixed on paper or in sound. A sense of the music or the story being out there, in the mix, as life rushes by, underpins our 'trusting search' for it.

I am not suggesting Beethoven was an insect. Nor am I trying to mechanise the mystery of how art comes to be. If anything, I wish to make it stranger, and truer, by the process of counter-intuition described earlier. We are not insects or birds, but we *are* animals, and all animals have their own way of transforming sense data into experience – what it is 'like' to be hungry, to feel pain, to hear sound or be (*pace* Thomas Nagel) a bat.

What I *am* suggesting is that artistic vision, far from being an inaccessible cultural refinement, is a part of our animal response to the world, which comes soon after the encounter with stimuli, and gives those stimuli meaning. Painters know this. From Cézanne onwards, the geometric re-sorting of fully apprehended objects like tables and plates into lines and discs has been a way of reminding us of what it is the eye actually sees before the mind gets to work on the sense data and turns them into items of furniture. The artist's need to discover the special aesthetic properties of an image, or a sound, is an extension of the mind's more fundamental need to discover form – to stabilise a relation between new stimuli and known objects. In that moment between exposure (to light, sound, pressure) and recognition, we are all animals – and artists.

This moment is a source of wonder. It is mercurial, always reproducing itself as the eye moves in saccades across the room – resolving one image and then the next – or as we find ourselves ambushed by the sheer attack of a songbird's melody, not yet having spotted the blackbird, or thrush, or robin pouring it into the air. And it is especially a musical encounter, I think, because it is an experience before it has a name or describes anything. This immediacy has much in common with the experience of childhood synaesthesia, where words and things and sounds (and self) are bound together. In *Flickerbook* (2006), her sensual memoir of early life in the Manchester of the 1920s and 30s, Leila Berg reinhabits the memory of pushing her way through autumn leaves: 'Crunching, whispering, scuttling leaves! Is it the leaves I am hearing or the words? Where have they come from, these words?'

So much of writing is the attempt to undo the separation of word and world so that we can 'see' the latter as we once knew it to be – and of course it cannot be done, even if you believe, as the Romantics did, that words are things. The poignancy of Berg's summoning lies in its refusal of the truth that the gap between experience and the moment of retrieval – of writing about it – widens as you get older, although really the gap is always there, because words refer beyond themselves as musical notes do not. If you write a piece of music inspired by your childhood, the notes say nothing about your age now or then. The paradox of music, even old music, is that it is a temporal art with no views on history. It insists only on being, which is why people like it at funerals.

During the recent Covid lockdowns, the importance of these 'musical' encounters was borne in on me by the two woodpigeons who arrived unexpectedly in my yard and their tough-nut cousins in the park. Finding myself bereft of normal objectives and destinations – going to work, going to see people – I paid attention to these common birds for what felt like the first time; looked, listened, experienced their oddity and familiarity; saw how the people coming to feed them – approaching singly, speculatively, seeking contact – made their own scattered flock. Like us, pigeons forage individually but imitate each other within a group, taking advantage of the same convenient food source and competing for it. One afternoon I saw a flock descend. Their fast, zig-zagging tussles over a few crumbs had a dramatic outcome: there was a fight (or what I call a fight: perhaps it was something less/more for the pigeons) and the loser flew off, retreated into one of the Lombardy poplars overlooking the upper pond.

I felt I was among the birds, and defined in relation to them, to their motion. I felt this as a musical property, something rhythmical. The vocal commotion, the head-bobbing, the stamping and fluffing and their rapid cessation seemed to stretch out one moment and disappear into the next with the changing light. Back home, the woodpigeons weighed heavily on the branches of my elder bush while looking away in different directions. They were at once intimately observable, and very hard to describe.

As I came to write 'Pigeon', a musical image on the scale of the pieces from Olivier Messiaen's *Petites esquisses d'oiseaux* (1985) – his last work for the piano and one of his most beautiful for that instrument – I had (unlike Messiaen) no initial sense that I would be writing 'about' birds. But I did see, without yet hearing, two and then three lines in simple time jerkily mimicking each other, moving in intervals, dovetailing, pulling apart, pausing now and again, before rushing forward, sometimes stumbling. Once I had that idea, the notes suggested themselves. I wrote them down and their clustering turned into a canon. (A canon is a form of counterpoint in which note-for-note repetitions of a melody overlap each other at various intervals and rhythmic distances; a round, for example, is a kind of canon.) At about that stage, I knew the motion was that of pigeons, scrapping and breaking off, and a kind of story fashioned itself from the notes' wordless conversation – that of a solitary bird being ousted or returning to its mate.

A reasonable objection to this account is that I am trying to have it both ways! First, I've said the shaping of the piece is intrinsically animal, then – halfway through writing it – the notes get identified with that-over-there and the music is suddenly 'about' or 'like' a pigeon coming adrift. In other words, a description. Well, which is it?

Leonard Bernstein (and he is not alone) raises a forceful objection to the idea that music refers to *any* externals in his NBC show for children, *What Does Music Mean?*, from 1958: 'Music just is. Music is notes, beautiful notes and sounds put together in such a way that we get pleasure out of listening to them, and that's all there is to it.' One of his examples is Modest Mussorgsky's *Pictures at an Exhibition*. Stories and paintings and birds are associated with the music only 'because the composer SAYS so'; you could have other stories or objects replacing the 'Great Gate of Kiev' (Bernstein nominates the Mississippi river) and the music would be just as passionate, chordal, great.

That's true, but one can get too dogmatic about this kind of thing. *West Side Story*, even without the book and lyrics, has a more than arbitrary relation to its first treatment by William Shakespeare, and 'associated' isn't a dirty word. Things and ideas pair up – the goldfinch outside, right now, sounds like a nearly defunct doorbell – and Aristotle thought that association either by experience or recall underpinned the ability to learn. Bernstein indulges in it himself: on the one hand, musical meaning is (he says) 'just' the 'movement ... from one note to another'; on the other hand, music '*names feelings* [my italics] only in notes instead of in words'. So it *does* describe (that is, it describes feelings). Can't both positions be true? A movement of notes takes us from abstraction to emotion. To hear just the bugler's first two notes in the Last Post is to have an experience, and experiences involve emotional associations. That's how we make sense of them.

The mystery of music isn't solved by putting it on some Platonic top shelf. It may not point to specific externals, but that is not to say it doesn't depend formatively on the world of other things, in a way most composers – including Tippett, Mozart, Schoenberg and Messiaen

– acknowledge. A comparison with mathematics is instructive. Would we have formed the concept of number without objects, like sheep, that needed to be counted? And would rhythm and melody have developed without our ancestors' awareness of the drumming of hooves, or the dawn chorus in the forest canopy?

Associations matter. Without them, where are we? Without them, where is the artistic possibility of imitation? Without them, Messiaen cannot claim of his vast, intricate piano cycle *Catalogue d'oiseaux* (1956–8) that 'All here is truth, even the countryside with its accompanying sights, sounds, smells and thermal currents.' Without them, Kate Bush's swooping melodic lines do not follow the motion of a kite (in 'Kite'). Without them, lyrics are arbitrary; we don't need Noël Coward's words, and Prince's erotic 'Tamborine' isn't a funny, sexy, teasing evocation. Without them, John Cage's '4'33"' is an absence, not a teeming presence. Without them, one note cannot suggest the next and there is no change, no 'questioning' (so: no Beethoven), no wondering 'what-now?' as you look at your hands in contrary motion on the keyboard and think of two spiders, a mirror, parting.

The truth is a kind of dissonance. Music isn't about anything, but it carries meaning: and, for some reason, this dissonance matters to me.

To answer the question at the head of this chapter, I work in a welter of associations, confronted by moving images and blurred auditory signals filling the landscape in front of me, and my job is to decide which ones count. I can't adequately convey what this is like in the moment of writing (either words or music); I can't tell you what I am about to do; I can't refer to the unconscious directly. But the sense of an objective (the house standing back from the road) becoming more stable, even as the foreground roils with near panic, is at the heart of it; I can only, like a sandpiper searching for the right tiny mollusc among so many inert shells, react consecutively to the lure of each note, each verbal relation. This way or that? Over here? Over there?

Did the idea of another bird lead to 'Sandpiper'? After 'Two Ornaments', I may have considered the possibility of pairing pieces like the panels of a diptych, but I suspect the mazy action of the second piece had multiple origins. It took a while to hatch as a bird.

Hitting the keyboard with both hands together and then alternating hands, as fast as you can go, is a staple of childhood play, which – to my ears – survives into both the finale of Mozart's Piano Sonata No. 8 in A Minor, K310, where the left hand hops about after the right, and the pulsating fifth dance in Bulgarian rhythm from the last book in Bartók's astonishing piano tutor, *Mikrokosmos*. But these were not conscious influences, and I am not sure who or what the finished piece resembles, musically. Andrzej Panufnik? Lene Lovich? All I know is that it led me to its own nature. There was a moment when it became a sandpiper, when the up-and-down 'teetering' turned into a gliding quest across the octaves, dipping into tonality – F sharp minor followed by a swerve into D minor in bars eighteen to twenty-one – before flying off again: and I knew what I had seen.

TWO BIRDS

for solo piano

TWO BIRDS

1. Pigeon

Pigeon

...breadcrumbs appear...

Poco più mosso

p *sub.*

...a fight breaks out...

mf ***f*** ***mf*** ***mp***

mp

tempo primo e rit.

...a single, hungry pigeon takes flight...

p *legato al fine*

molto rit.

pp

ppp

breve

...the light changes.

mf

April 30th, 2022

2. Sandpiper

"Poor bird, he is obsessed!" —Elizabeth Bishop

Sandpiper

May 1st, 2022

5.

A therapist friend of mine likes to talk about the importance of artistic freedom, of being attuned to the unconscious, and letting creative difficulties solve themselves organically. 'Or not at all,' I once said, a bit gloomily, though fairly. Because this is what the creative-writing and motivational-instructional schools of thinking leave out: the inevitability of disappointment, of being stymied by constraints (no time, no ideas, no money), and the reality of failure. The organicist creed also ignores a fact of professional life, which is that if someone does give you money or a contract to write something, you had better do it. You won't go to jail if you don't, but nor will you feel good about yourself. And then, even when you do get down to it, you will run aground and panic.

Some of us worry more than others; for what it's worth, I believe this fear of failure has to do with formative relationships in which expectations that had nothing to do with you were made to have something to do with you. But the only answer to that legacy, in adulthood, is doggedness and energised patience; to remember the reason you started making and wondering in the first place, which was to exert some mastery over your environment: what is this light in the sky, and what is it like if I put my fingers over it?

Professionals differ from good amateurs in one or two key respects only. They are paid, and they have managed to master others' expectations while retaining a sense of freedom in execution and invention. Their attitude to failure is almost complaisant: it is unavoidable and necessary. Your job, as an artist (as a composer once told me), is to make triumphs of mistakes, and you do this by staying the course. Have therapy, if you would like it, but do not run crying to your *work* about your psychological wounds. They are your material and where, frankly, would you be without them?

For a long time now I have taken medication for two related difficulties: pain and anxiety. I reserve the right to be bullish about them, borne aloft on a low but sufficiently elevating dose of Zoloft. If you don't need chemical assistance, great. If you are in serious difficulties, and larger doses don't seem to touch the problem, then I sympathise, because I think I know what that is like. Wait, if you can.

If you are not a professional, behave as if you were. Be disciplined. The 'as if' in life, as someone says in *Murmur*, is crucial. In my experience it is the practical solution to terror and the fear that you will lose your mind: behave as if you will not. Certain of my acquaintances may consider the loss to have occurred a while ago, but that possibility may itself be conceded under the self-preserving terms of the course of action prescribed: 'I will assume that it has not and proceed accordingly.' The 'as if' tactic covers most related anxieties about competency, too. Only geniuses know if they are talented, and even then they may be deluded, because talent, like kindness or any other practical virtue, cannot be claimed. It is not possessed. It is simply demonstrated and characteristic, so why not assume the possibility of its existence, however residual?

When I say 'wait', I am not speaking idly in the what-will-be-will-be organicist mode, which promises either easeful achievement or nothing at all. This is not the counsel of despair; it is the opposite. It is really an instruction to accept circumstances by observing particulars; to blink and refocus. A patient of Jung's wrote him a letter saying, 'I always thought that when we accepted things they overpowered us in some way or other. This turns out not to be true at all, and it is only by accepting them that one can assume an attitude towards them.' He goes on to say that this acceptance is a kind of alternation, between states good and bad, promising and indifferent, a sort of unification by oscillation. In my own case, I have found unusual solutions to apparently insoluble personal and artistic problems by halting one activity (writing) entirely and taking up another (music), before returning to the first problem; the turning away is acceptance of a special kind, as if I were saying, 'Well, that is so, and I cannot do any more about it at present, so now I will do *this* instead. I will find whatever is amenable to development. I will assume an attitude towards things.'

This attitude is by definition unstable, restless as well as accepting, but what drives it is the need to turn a difficulty or an imaginative crisis to account; to make a separate thing of the disordering mental encounter with pain or beauty, which Michael Tippett calls an 'ineffable experience' and W. H. Auden a 'passion of awe'. The accusation levied at this kind of self-distraction is that it produces dilettantism; that it leads to scattiness, even a kind of morally irresponsible shallowness, the trifling with skill that Jane Austen amusedly observes in her creation Emma Woodhouse: 'She played and sang; – and drew in almost every style; but steadiness had always been wanting; and in nothing had she approached the degree of excellence which she would have been glad to command, and ought not to have failed of.'

Brilliant as Austen's judgement may be, it shares in Emma's own blindness insofar as it describes only the disappointments of an ambition that is social: the desire to *seem* accomplished. If Emma had needed to *be* an artist, to respond to inner promptings as Tippett and Auden did, then the desire to 'do everything' would not have mattered. Her drawings and her playing would have entailed each other as the poles entail the Earth, and her failures would have been absorbed into that search for an artistic product of emotion that proceeds by leaving behind the 'niggardly part of the ego', as Flannery O'Connor put it, and judging everything, even intense personal discord, with a stranger's eye. The difficulty, whatever it is, must be owned by being held at arm's length. This is also the Socratic method, deepening one's understanding by questioning it.

The division of artistic interests, like the presence of competing desires, does not imply a want of seriousness or concentration. It implies a whole person. You cannot talk sensibly about 'multiple selves' at a non-pathological level; it's just a glamorous metaphor. The point about the different aspects of a personality, artistic or otherwise, is that they belong to one person. And the point about, for example, the proliferating personae of a writer like the Portuguese poet and critic Fernando Pessoa, who wrote under many names – Ricardo Reis, Alberto Caeiro, Álvaro de Campos are the main ones – is that they belong to the same writer. Similarly, in a piece of work one is not seeking to magic up variety for its own sake but to help disparate actions, voices, timbres, feelings and influences discover the principle that holds them together.

We return to the idea of association or complementarity – dialogue – which art, as the combination of inner and outer realities, can hardly do without. If you set a disordering experience or imaginative insight at a slight distance, in order to understand it properly, your attitude to it becomes one of inquiry. What you are doing, then, is modelling the discomfort or the tune or the scene you have in your head, trying to ask open questions that turn it from a point of distraction into a point of interest. 'Listen, what is this, and what are you? Can I move a fraction this way or in some other way?' The attitude one adopts is that of someone asking a wiser person to guide them by example, and it's at this level, sensitively, probably unconsciously, that artistic models and influences make themselves felt. I grew up with the classical repertoire while listening to the American jazz composer Carla Bley (who died last year), because my father always had her playing in his room – and I loved her warm waywardness, all hard collisions, sforzandos and sudden passionate melody. Bley's big-band sound is a fusion of modern jazz and the surreal avant-garde – Erik Satie and Charles Mingus were her heroes – but the way it unfolds is oddly interrogatory: every phrase says, 'Not just this, but that, and maybe *that*, too.' A bit like Haydn.

In a conversation with Frank J. Oteri for the online journal *NewMusicBox*, Bley says: 'Right now [2003] I'm working on a piece that so far has two parts. First it had one part, but then it suggested going somewhere else ... So I wrote another part. But then I thought, "This wants to go back to the first part." So I thought maybe Part One should be Part Two, but then I thought I'd need an introduction. I just ask myself all these questions as I'm sitting there or lying in the tub. This is my process: asking questions.' And that, too, is how I arrived at 'Toccatina', which was originally a half-page sketch abandoned in the late 1980s. Its moment came when I'd finished 'Two Ornaments' and 'Two Birds' and felt a kind of binary form coming on – two pieces that could speak to each other, without interpenetrating, in the manner of a diptych. A diptych is a two-panelled painting, but in the ancient world it was also the equivalent of an exercise book: two wax plates facing each other on which you wrote or drew with a stylus. The wax could then be heated, and the work erased or remade.

'Toccatina' (small toccata) is a piece achieved by questioning and erasure. The toccata ('act of touching') was a flamboyant solo baroque form originally brought to perfection on the keyboard in Germany by the young J. S. Bach, though its characteristic multi-sectioned virtuosity has survived in the idea of impromptus (like Schubert's, No. 2 in E Flat Major, D899, my favourite, with its glissades of triplets) and any number of fantasies and études from the nineteenth century. Delicacy as well as dexterity is indispensable to a real toccata, however. It can't just be showy; it has to be something touch-sensitive, intricate, its different sections shaped by call-and-response (think of the Toccata and Fugue in D Minor, BWV 565), like an argumentative couple falling out and getting back together again. Call-and-response is also what makes it jazzy.

When I came back to the half-page sketch, I saw in it a resemblance to a ferocious three-minute Carla Bley number called 'Real Life Hits', a series of angular statements by the full band with clever use of tied notes, swing accents, pauses and little runs to suggest three-note rhythms where it's really all 4/4. The solo sections take you in a different direction, almost towards bossa nova. It's very athletic, with a forceful unison ending – in B flat, where you've been all along without realising it. My piece was too four-square by comparison – subject in G, then echo in D, then a second motif derived from the first and a similar pattern of imitation – so I took it apart, bar by bar, stretched it, and put it back together. What Bley gave me was the freedom to concentrate on one idea: that notes delivered at pace, like jiggling atoms, can make up different 'molecular' groupings. Six quavers together can sound like three groups of two or two groups of three. Or a group of four can be a group of three with one left over, according to how hard you land on the last note. This matter of emphasis unlocked the middle section for me. It sounds different to the first two pages, though it's just the result of me asking, 'How can I get something new out of the main theme?' Answer: by holding it at a rhythmical distance.

The 'third' section is an accelerated merging of the first two parts – the angular subject and the driving middle section – with some passagework and a sense of the whole piece both coming together and rewinding until it vanishes completely, like a toy universe collapsing in on itself. I pinched this idea, semi-deliberately, from Beethoven, whose incredible and ultra-economical rondo finale to the Piano Sonata No. 7 in D Major, Op. 10, No. 3 asks an upward-inflected question (three notes: 'Is this it?') that lasts the entire movement, makes you wait and wait for the answer – given in a sort of forgiving trance across four bars and nine chords on the last page – and then, at the far end of the street, as it were, turns a corner into magical silence.

What my too-brief homage to LVB and Bley (and Bach) doesn't have is a gentle bit, a lyrical pause. I wondered about putting one in, wrote it and dropped the notion. Sometimes the missing element in a story or a musical statement is a separate statement, or something that belongs alongside a piece without existing inside it. I'd half hoped I would write a second toccatina (to make

'Two Toccatinas'), because I like the toccata's self-assembling, flexible form, and felt unduly confident another one would come along, since work often gives rise to more work in the same vein. 'Paintings breed,' says Bridget Riley, and she's right – except, of course, that offspring have a habit of surprising their parents by not being anything like them.

'Luf-Daungere' is the more deeply engraved panel of the diptych. It comes out of not knowing, at all, what might be possible after the pleasure of writing 'Toccatina'. That rare experience of feeling I knew what I was doing – interrogating a sketch and using it to build something new – didn't repeat itself; I couldn't, after all, turn a routine into a method. And when I asked myself, 'What next?' which I often do, particularly if I haven't slept and am in pain, I didn't get an answer. Or rather, I did, but the answer to my petition was in the negative. Sometimes the answer is a shadow, a failure, and that has to be enough: 'Luf-Daungere' is a medieval compound word, found in *Pearl*, the beautiful fourteenth-century lament for a lost daughter, written (it is assumed) by the author of *Sir Gawain and the Green Knight*. Love-Danger expresses the two-sidedness of one's deepest, truest love for someone, who is indispensable to you, whom you lose. The piece is a series of slow-moving chords from which a chant escapes. In its own idiomatic way, it *is* another toccatina, because it has miniature call-and-response sections separated by chorale-like measures. It also represents a kind of priority for me – learning to be still – so that, though I wrote it after the showier piece, it had to come first.

When you have nothing, you may still have something. Or, as my consultant Charlotte likes to say, 'If it's not one thing, it's another.' Charlotte's great. She doesn't get too involved. She's professionally interested in me and very caring, I think. She just isn't merged with my predicament. She can contemplate it, in other words, and that is what one is trying to do with experience, artistically – avoid being merged with it, so that it can be made available to others, so that the resulting idiom is personal but not private, a painful difficulty to which further inquiry is the only realistic answer.

TWO IDIOMS

for solo piano

TWO IDIOMS

1. Luf-Daungere

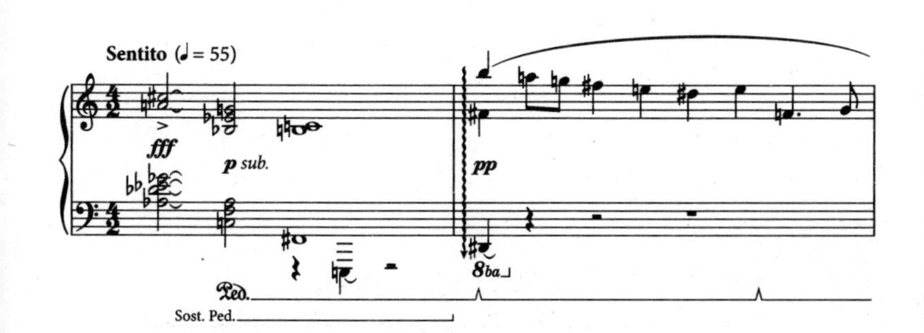

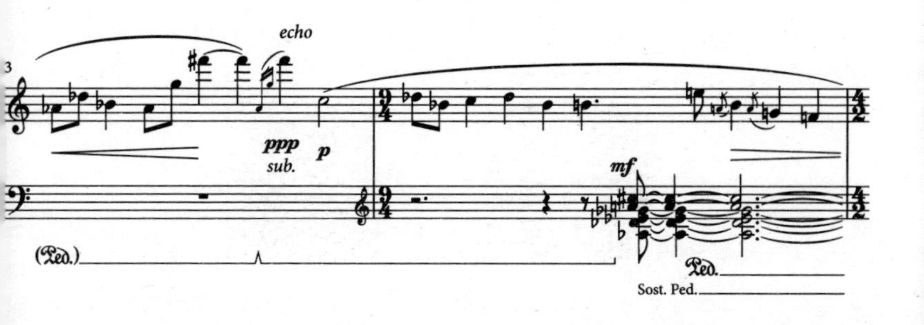

Luf-Daungere

2. Toccatina

Toccatina

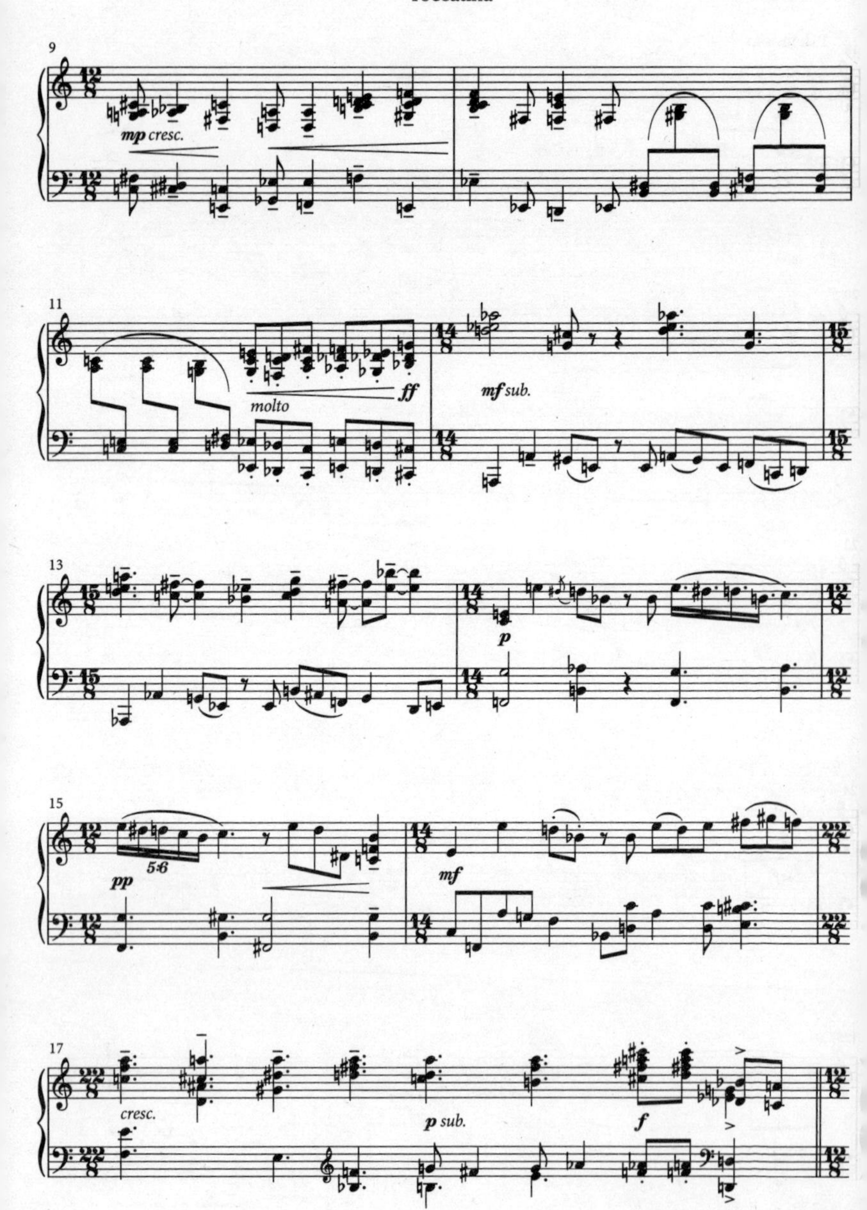

Toccatina

Toccatina

Toccatina

July 16th, 2022

6.

The last panel of these *Four Diptychs* is a belated companion piece for the galliard with which we started – a pavan, the stately processional dance of the Renaissance and early baroque, cast in duple time; a form that leans on the first half of the bar as the dancers join hands or rise onto their toes, and then relaxes into movement.

The word 'pavan' is a strange evolution of 'Padua', in which Italian city the dance possibly originated, and in its later incarnation as a staple of consort (small ensemble) music it retains a sense of longing for some lost point of origin. The great pavans of the period are moving and questing constructions, often in three movements or 'strains', sometimes bearing a patron's name, sometimes intended as memorials. William Byrd and Orlando Gibbons both wrote dedicatory pavans ('Pavana: The Earl of Salisbury' and 'The Lord of Salisbury, his Pavin'), which appear in a famous book of early keyboard music called *Parthenia* (1612), and Gibbons's downwards-flowing theme in its turn recalls the tear-shaped 'Lachrimae

Pavan' (1600) by the lutenist John Dowland. Probably the most famous latter-day example of this dance is Ravel's early piano piece, 'Pavane pour une infante défunte' (1899), which has melancholy and charm in equal measure. It can be played too slowly. When the pianist Charles Oulmont performed it, Ravel apparently said, 'Next time remember that I wrote a pavan for a dead princess, not a dead pavan for a princess ...'

I cannot claim these forebears as models. The simpler truth seems to be that the pavan answers to my temperament, which is drawn to meditations, the tension between public demonstration and introspection that helps define, for me, the appeal of music-making and composition. The 'strains' that make up a pavan are not-quite repetitions, not-quite variations; and yet somehow, when you reach the last chord, you feel you have travelled very far indeed. The return home is never nostalgic. Rather it is sharpened by a new interior awareness of a trusting search come good. The ornaments and contrapuntal knick-knacks picked up on your travels turn out to be precious and foundational. They belong. If there were an epigram to go with every pavan ever written, it would be either 'Let us run with patience the race that is set before us' or 'The stone which the builders rejected, the same is become the head of the corner'.

Pavans, like chaconnes, have an infinite quality. Getting the point of them is not a matter of haste but of alertness, being balanced, primed to receive and value an impression. They do not provide answers, and I love art that avoids answers, because it tells me there isn't a better way of living my life than the one I have chosen or am choosing, just many different ways of valuing what happens to me.

Let me offer two images to illustrate this odd business of valuation.

My weather eye for distraction is based on the belief that, as I have tried to suggest, one's peripheral artistic vision and secondary activities – in my case music – are actually essential fields of enquiry. You must catch, and prize, things as they occur to you. Photographs are like this – a mixture of the intended but provisional, the spontaneously meant – and I am haunted by the loss of one in particular, which showed me as a boy of seven lying at my mother's feet in a park. I think the park was Sydney Gardens in Bath. I can still hear a passing train in the background and, nearer, the copper beech trees. Who took it? I suppose it must have been my father, who worked nearby. We went home; the moment passed. The picture was developed, put in an envelope (perhaps it was too big for an album?) and handed down to me. I gave it to a paper to illustrate an article and it was not returned. I'm sorry about the mislaying of that photograph, because it was a lovely composition, and because its fled intensity says something to me about the nature of sincere emotions, like compassion and generous interest, which aren't constant feelings but rather swiftly taken opportunities.

The other image is of a sixth-form disco, in 1984 it must have been. Now, I didn't have many crushes at school. It wasn't that kind of school. And at the beginning of the AIDS pandemic, faced with the hysteria of the public advertisements, I felt that the safest route through adolescence was to remain an observer a while longer – but I did really like one boy who, to my surprise, asked me if I wanted to dance. Was he asking me to dance, or did he just not want to venture out onto the dance floor (our common room) on his own? The latter. Anyway, I said no, because, when he asked his question, half seriously, half joking, I was talking to some other friends, among whom were a number of girls I'd started to get to know, through parents and after-school activities, at parties, in pubs that turned a blind eye to our evident youth. We mounted plays wearing curtains and jumble. Sang in choirs. This boy wouldn't have known what to make of any of that. He wasn't part of any set, though he and I had always been friendly. He wore soft-collar shirts and shaved his neck raw. He stuck his hands in his pockets and wandered off. The girls laughed, as if his question could be taken to mean something, their laughter not unkind or mocking, but frustrated, uncomprehending, not knowing where to put itself. And I wanted to say,

'Stop!' before he passed through the double doors, and to run after him. 'Good idea. We ought to dance. I'll dance with you.' Because, if I had, my whole life might have been very little altered, certainly that evening, but for the knowledge that I'd said 'yes' when I wanted to, and all that such knowledge entails.

These images have a relation to the work I have chosen to do – writing – because I know it can be hard to keep hold of things or to say yes to someone. And vice versa.

I said no to the piano at about the time I left school. And I think I said no in the same slightly confused and fearful spirit as I said no to that dance, because I knew the piano was something I loved – that it was a friend. I say 'confused' because I did not yet know the value of that friend, and because I had the sense that if I chose it wholeheartedly, then it would probably reject me. I would not turn out to be any good at it.

What would I say to my seventeen-year-old self, now, if I had the chance? I hope I would not try to provide answers. I would say nonetheless: the danger with being persuaded against doing what you want to do when young is that life will do its best as you get older to make you forget what it was. Tony Bennett was a great singer in part because he never declined the chance to practise a discipline that brought him pleasure. Hokusai counselled young artists to find something they enjoyed doing and to keep doing it.

I would also say: for all the artists who have known their vocation, just as many have *not* known, or have doubted it. My belief is that you should not expect to know what it is you can do; that there is an ancient and insoluble contradiction involved in the idea of freely creating and knowing in advance what it is one can make. The American abstract artist Stuart Davis said: 'I did not spring into the world ready equipped to paint the kinds of things I have wanted to paint.' James Baldwin echoed him: 'Beyond talent lie all the usual words: discipline, love, luck, but most of all, endurance.' To find out anything, one needs to cultivate an enduringly sceptical self-reliance.

Paul Hunter, the actor-director who runs the theatre company Told by an Idiot, told me that he made himself act by throwing himself at the challenge. The decision looked very risky in the early 1980s, from his working-class parents' point of view, but Paul knew that, as he put it, 'if I gave myself a fallback option, I would fall back on it'.

I can see that. Just as I can see, and know from experience, that the second-resort love may be the satisfying one, because it comes less naturally and forces you to adapt. Perhaps, too, the relegation of a fulfilling activity to the margins of a busy life preserves that activity's wonder and importance so that it can be taken up later. It may even be that Plato was right and that this reawakening of memory, which he called *anamnesis*, is the root of all human learning.

Within the practice of music, the constant reawakening of memory is indispensable. Brilliance of execution and vocation, as a performer or a composer, necessarily conceal the foundations on which such things rest. I am thinking about the labour it takes to achieve and maintain technique, the solid grasp of harmony that allows a musician to improvise, and the ordinary pervasiveness – the accepted value – of musical culture that makes possible the emergence of a major figure. If, for example, we let the glare of Franz Liszt's concert-hall achievement fade for a moment, we see the domestic music-making and the return to private meditation on which his late works depended. The composer Alexander Borodin (whose main career was as a chemist) heard Liszt play as an old man, in 1883, and acclaimed a pianism that 'astounded me with its remarkable simplicity, sobriety and austerity ... his tempos are moderate, not exaggerated, he never bridles up. And yet: What an abundance of energy, passion, dedication and fire – in spite of his age!'

With Liszt, as with Chopin, the mistake is to be bamboozled by virtuosity, which is *not* complexity. Oscar Peterson was a technically superb jazz pianist, and a tenth as interesting as Thelonious Monk. After the wild display comes the realisation that the less adorned the musical line, the greater the challenge to the player to capture its implications – to make us hear all that is contained by a single phrase, cell or note. The argument can even be made that one of Liszt's most difficult pieces is the ultra-spare 'Nuages gris' (1881) – a tone poem in miniature that presages both the serial revolution of the Second Viennese School and the proto-minimalism of Erik Satie, but which is also heavy with the implication of all that came before it. The contrapuntal turn halfway through this short composition falls on the ear like a vault door swinging slowly open: the 'past isn't even past' (William Faulkner); it is still rich with promise.

Improvisation pushes that door wide open. It is often written about as if it were a liberation from constraint and stuffy staves. No: it is the result of rehearsal. It belongs with the process of composition. It may be free of notation, but it's still planned in the sense that it is determined by a harmonic framework that has been absorbed by the player. Music isn't a miracle. Like the operations of free will, improvised music has multiple contingent circumstances, from the training of the pianist, to the touch of the keyboard being used and the acoustic of the hall, to the memory of devices that have worked in the past. Equally, a good amount of engraved eighteenth- and nineteenth-century music alludes to its improvisatory origins – voluntaries, impromptus, intermezzi, preludes – in part to give the impression of inspired casualness, of being superbly dashed off, but also to show that composition may itself be thought of as a provisional act, because it leads back to more, and more varied, performances.

The last and most important thing I would say to my seventeen-year-old self would be to advise him to banish the fear of first steps, the journey ahead, of failing, and to be amused by his pretensions as soon as they are discovered. When Beethoven looked at one of Schlösser's compositions, he was good-humoured about it. 'You have put too much into it, less would have been better,' he said happily. 'That is due to youth, always ready to take Heaven by storm, always afraid of not having done enough, but I'm sure that a riper age will remedy this.' What a great thing to say! I haven't that excuse – my pieces are too dense, too short, and I'm not young – but the lesson, of the good being in there somewhere, predicated on the not-so-good, is well taken.

And its corollary, at the level of culture and attainment, is that although artists of lasting merit are always in short supply, and time decides who they are, this in no way diminishes the importance of lesser contributors, the readers, the tweeters, the hobbyist painters and poets, the amateur singers and players and senders of funny cards, who fill out the rest of the creative continuum. 'Importance' is putting it too meanly: these people are essential. If I go to the park, I do not go to see bacteria in the soil, and yet without those bacteria there would be no flowers or trees.

In the biome of culture, minor poets and musicians and composers and painters are indispensable. We should believe Virginia Woolf on this score, rather than Louis MacNeice, whose 'Elegy for Minor Poets' is a masterpiece of misdirection ('Are you insinuating that you are a Minor Poet, Louis?' 'God, no.'). Woolf is more modest, more positive, and more accurate. In her essay 'The Elizabethan Lumber Room', she addresses Shakespeare's forgotten contemporaries. These vanished dramatists and poets are not lost to us. Rather, they have been taken up, like nutrients, into the vascular system of a still-growing art form. All artists are voyagers, she says: 'One expedition might fail, but what if the passage to the fabled land ... lay only a little further up the coast?'

What we should *never* do is dishonour the attempt to make art – always difficult, especially when we are trying to be simple – by pretending that difficulty and application and skill are of no account; that if it seems too hard, we shouldn't bother with it. If trees need soil, then seedlings need the shelter of trees – the protection of examples, and the encouragement of a teacher. But a lot of trees are being cut down.

I learned the oboe and the violin from peripatetic teachers who turned up in the damp and infested music block every Friday. In Britain today, very few children without money in the family will learn a musical instrument. Most secondary schools no longer provide such lessons. Those children who learn an instrument privately, and attain a high degree of proficiency thereby, are treated as miraculous outgrowths, prodigies of self-invention, their clear economic advantages in a supposed lottery of talent carefully misrepresented. The panicky response of broadcasters and charitable foundations to structural inequality is 1) to lie by omission ('Here are the young people that we have decided to support, *ergo* young people are being supported'); 2) to be critically unreliable when it comes to the work of the historically under-represented (conflating sex with tonalism, for instance, in the neglect of a composer like Dorothy Howell, 1898–1982); 3) to appear to work hard at welcoming in others without giving up their own window seats. It's patronising. But it's easier to do than face the reality of the way an entire political generation has calmly divested poorer children of their right to an education. The result, in music, is that there is a kind of embargo on the public discussion – on air – of technical matter. You are advised not to speak of notation, as if it didn't exist. Not to say the words 'sonata form' ('That's a big red flag,' as one industry chief said to me). And to treat the grammar of any artistic discipline as something fearful and prohibitive.

The acquisition of grammatical skill – the ability to read and notate music – does not constrain expression or exclude people in principle, any more than the Highway Code constrains learner drivers. But the reluctance to teach it, the fear of owning it as a liberating experience, and the political aversion to making art in general a serious object of study – all these things are indeed constraints, and highly exclusionary.

Music, in *all* its forms, notated or not, takes everyone seriously. That is why I have included the scores of my pieces written alongside this essay. Populism (and the prejudice against notation and the opportunity to learn a technical aesthetic skill are populist moves) does not take anyone seriously; quite the reverse. It befogs the real agenda, which is controlling. To say, to some unspecified imaginary mass audience, that 'crotchets are naff' may sound inviting and jokily reassuring, but all it achieves (possibly all it intends) is the consolidation of a hierarchy at the expense of curiosity, which is our universal birthright. The people who know notes and staves already get to keep their knowledge, and those who don't are persuaded it isn't for the likes of them.

The promulgation of this notion is widespread and a reflection, in this country, of a deeper reactionary turn away from the post-war settlement, which sought to make education detailed and comprehensive.

I am more sorry than angry, and I am angry enough. The past may finally be past if we are not careful. All it takes is for one generation to grow up without the ability to notate – the mnemonic skill that allows us to extend our capacity to remember notes, to conserve pieces beyond the limits of normal memory – and that skill will be gone, and with it the keys to the vast treasure house of written music.

PAVAN

for solo piano

PAVAN

Pavan

7.

I am nearly at the end of this short account of a period spent composing for the piano. I have finished the *Four Diptychs* – in fact, I finished them a while ago. Were they just a distraction from fiction and poetry? Or something more? They were not easy to come up with, exactly, but they had momentum and that peculiar self-command that takes a grateful creator by surprise, even as the 'catch' becomes clear: there may be no way back 'in' to such work once *it* has finished with *you*. The essay has taken longer to write and has been disconcerting, even upsetting, to assemble. It has involved an encounter with memory and looking again that I have not enjoyed so much, although of course it, too, has revealed its purpose, which is that of returning me to the workshop. A place where the obstacles and limitations of prose are at least somewhat known to me.

A word more is needed about ease and difficulty, which exist both as aesthetic properties of art and as experiences of its execution. The property and the experience tend to get mixed up together and are worth disentangling.

I have said that the *Diptychs*, most of them, came to me relatively easily. That is so. However, their shared flaw is undoubtedly the kind of 'difficult' compression to which Beethoven was alluding in his remarks to Schlösser. I can't help but hear voices from my own past as I think about this – the teachers and friends who have always told me I am being too difficult. Sometimes I agree with them. At others I stick to my guns, enlisting Albert Einstein's famous, possibly apocryphal, remark that a theorem should be 'as simple as possible *but no simpler*'. The destiny of a work of art is to realise its own implications, and sometimes that means accepting their complexity.

Simplicity, on the other hand, is rarely what it seems.

As a young journalist, I got tongue-tied in front of the film director Lewis Gilbert (a lovely man) and he was kind. 'Ask the simple question,' he said. Then again, a few weeks ago, listening to the radio, I heard the musician Ben Watt (one half of Everything But the Girl) saying he took comfort from Nadia Boulanger's advice that one should 'never be afraid to be simple'. My music teacher, the organist Peter Jezard, wrote in a school report: 'William is apt to think the answers to questions more difficult than they really are.' I remember at the time thinking that this bit of headshaking was unfair. If the answer hadn't occurred to me (and I wasn't deliberately avoiding it), how was it simple? Or: if it was in me, somewhere, but I'd forgotten it, then clearly something had to be worked through in order for me to be recalled to simplicity.

The fact is that simplicity is hard and hidden. You would love to know why or how something is so extraordinary, and you may never know; there may be no answer. Stonehenge and the *Notebooks for Anna Magdalena Bach* (1722, 1725) are inexplicable. And Boulanger's advice, taken the wrong way, can be disastrous, because it can lead people to equate simplicity with facility – either to think their instincts are infallible or to believe that, after years of labour, they have earned the right to a skill. No one has any right to skill. There are no such rights. Interestingly, writers who meet with success do sometimes forget this (I have heard a few of them talk about a thing called 'technical command'), whereas musicians and composers hardly ever do.

Simple is the wrong word. What the above counsellors mean is: say the *true* thing; the thing you really hear, see and think. And that is difficult, because it takes a good amount of searching and sifting – like the bee moving around the flower – to be sure of it, to achieve true clarity, which is never clear for long because life, as the medium in which we all work, admits of simplicity only as an ideal. Complications arise.

The true gesture may come about as a result of inspiration or after much study. The two tempi belong together. In *Human, All Too Human*, Friedrich Nietzsche, the greatest philosopher of music who has ever lived, explains that it is hard work and preparation that underpin sudden achievement and creative illumination. Artistic improvisation, he says, 'stands low in relation to artistic thoughts earnestly and laboriously chosen' (his example of an earnest and laborious chooser is Beethoven); and again, 'when productive energy has been dammed up for a while ... there is finally a sudden outpouring, as if a direct inspiration with no previous inner working out ... were taking place'. This is undoubtedly true, though perhaps it is even truer that the process of preparation and release is cyclical; that the unanticipated 'inspiration', while assuredly the product of 'rejecting, sifting, reforming, arranging', can also open up new territory for long-term habitation and development.

What matters, says Nietzsche, is the *power of judgement* (his italics). A shame, then, that one cannot always power one's way to the exercising of that judgement. Sometimes discernment must come by relaxing one's grip on the plan, the calling, the aesthetic orthodoxy, even the anti-orthodoxy. (Something has gone wrong, for example, when a revolutionary mode of expression begins to seem predictable – a problem familiar, in different ways, to purists of atonal music or free-jazz pioneers or anti-establishment comedians who become extremely popular.) What seems to be required, in the end, is a relaxation of the vocational self and a reintegration of different aspects of the artistic personality, the deliberate and the unpremeditated, which in turn signifies something deeper still – a new 'centre of gravity', Jung called it, 'no longer in the ego ... but in the hypothetical point between conscious and unconscious'.

This reintegration involves a hospitality to doubt that I recognise as one of my main preoccupations. A lot of life is hard, and at times I have doubted my commitment to it. But under the spotlight of attention paid to the hardest parts, it has yielded moments – short periods of creative delight – in which my awareness is heightened even as my self-consciousness disappears. Just as music means without describing, so my dialogue with it is intimate without being subjective. The simple thing? I do not have to explain myself at the keyboard. The 'I' dissolves. To sit at the piano and play middle C is to hear an instrument, and to feel myself, moving towards the fulfilment of fresh purpose.

These moments, at a slant to intention, are what make art surprising and life worth living. What they give me is the capacity to strike on regardless: courage, in a word. Courage is what I have found at the point of distraction.

Will Eaves, 22 August 2023

Some recommended listening

1.

Johann Sebastian Bach (1685–1750): *The Art of Fugue* BWV1080, 1751

Angela Hewitt, piano. *The Art of Fugue*. Hyperion CDA67980, 2013; Joanna MacGregor, piano. *Counterpoint: Art of Fugue/Canons and Studies by Conlon Nancarrow*. Collins Classics 70432, 1996

Frédéric Chopin (1810–49): Étude Op. 10, No. 1 in C Major, 1829

Tamás Vásáry, piano. *Frédéric Chopin: Waltzes, Études*. DG 2721 208, 1965/1979

Frédéric Chopin: Préludes Op. 28, 1829–39

Maurizio Pollini, piano. *Chopin: 24 Préludes Op. 28*. DG 2530 550, 1974

Benjamin Britten (1913–76): *Peter Grimes*, 1945

Peter Pears et al; Benjamin Britten conducting the Royal Opera House Orchestra and Chorus. *Peter Grimes*. Decca 475 7713, 1958

Harrison Birtwistle (1934–2022): *Gawain*, 1991
François Le Roux et al; Elgar Howarth, conducting the Royal Opera House Orchestra and Chorus. *Gawain*. Collins Classics 70412, 1996

John Dowland (1562/3–1626): Captain Piper's Pavan and Galliard (from Thomas Morley's *First Book of Consort Lessons*, 1599)
The Morley Consort, directed by David Munrow. *Two Renaissance Dance Bands*. EMI HQS 1249, 1971

John Dowland: The Frog Galliard ('Now, O now I needs must part', c.1597), transcribed for keyboard by Anon.
Colin Tilney, harpsichord. *John Dowland: The Collected Works*. L'Oiseau Lyre 452 563-2, 1976–80

Will Eaves (1967-): 'Galliard', 2022
Richard Uttley, piano. [https://soundcloud.com/richard_uttley/sets/will-eaves-the-point-of-distraction]

2.

Marc Shaiman (1959–): 'The Place Where Lost Things Go' (from *Mary Poppins Returns*, 2018)
Emily Blunt, vocal. *Mary Poppins Returns* (Original Soundtrack). Walt Disney Records D002693002, 2018

Hélène de Montgeroult (1764–1836): Études (from *Cours complet pour l'enseignement du fortpiano comprenant 114 études*, 1788–1812)
Clare Hammond, piano. *Hélène de Montgeroult: Études*. BIS 2603, 2022

Maurice Duruflé (1902–86): Prélude et Fugue sur le nom d'Alain, Op. 7, 1942
John Scott, organ. *The Complete Organ Music of Maurice Duruflé*. Hyperion CDA66368, 1990

Harold Arlen (1905–86): 'Over the Rainbow' (from *The Wizard of Oz*, 1939)
Judy Garland, vocal. *The Wizard of Oz* (Original Soundtrack). Rhino R2 71999, 1995

Prince (1958–2016): 'I No' and 'Alphabet Street' (from *Lovesexy*, 1988)
Prince, vocals and all arrangements. *Lovesexy*. Paisley Park 925 7201, 1988

Will Eaves: 'Carillon', 1990/2022
Sibelius digital organ track. [https://www.willeaves.com/blog]

3.

Erich Wolfgang Korngold (1897–1957): 'The Sea Hawk' (from *The Sea Hawk*, 1940)
William Stromberg, conducting the Moscow Symphony Orchestra. *The Sea Hawk and Deception*. Naxos 8.570110-11, 2007

Erich Wolfgang Korngold: 'Main Title' (from *The Adventures of Robin Hood*, 1939)
William Stromberg, conducting the Moscow Symphony Orchestra. *The Adventures of Robin Hood*. Naxos 8.573369, 2003

Stevie Wonder (1950–), 'Superstition' (from *Talking Book*, 1972)

Stevie Wonder. *Talking Book*. Tamla T 319L, 1972

Igor Stravinsky (1882–1971): *The Rite of Spring*, 1913

Valery Gergiev, conducting the Kirov Orchestra. *Stravinsky: The Rite of Spring* (with *Le poème de l'extase* by Alexander Scriabin). Phillips 468 035-2, 2001

Donna Summer (1948–2012): 'I Feel Love' (from *I Remember Yesterday*, 1977)

Donna Summer, vocal; Giorgio Moroder, Pete Bellotte. *I Remember Yesterday*. Casablanca NBLP 7056, 1977

Nicholas Britell (1980–): 'Succession – Main Title Theme' (from *Succession*, 2018–23)

Nicholas Britell. *Succession: Season 1 (HBO Original Series Soundtrack)*. Milan M2-37094, 2019

Johann Sebastian Bach: 'Chaconne' (from Partita for violin No. 2 in D Minor, BWV 1004, 1717–20)

Arthur Grumiaux, violin. *J.S. Bach: Complete Sonatas and Partitas for Solo Violin*. Phillips 438 736-2, 1961/1994

George Frideric Handel (1685–1759): 'Passacaille' (from Suite for harpsichord No. 7 in G Minor, HWV 432, 1720)

Danny Driver, piano. *The Eight Great Suites*. Hyperion CDA68041/2, 2014

Henry Purcell (1659–95): 'When I Am Laid in Earth' (from *Dido and Aeneas*, c.1683–88)
Janet Baker, soprano; English Chamber Orchestra conducted by Anthony Lewis. *Dido and Aeneas*. Decca 466 387-2, 1961/2000

Domenico Scarlatti (1685–1757): Sonata in G minor, K8, 1738
Alexandre Tharaud, piano. *Alexandre Tharaud plays Scarlatti*. Erato 6420162, 2011

Will Eaves: Two Ornaments from *Four Diptychs*, 2022
Richard Uttley, piano. [https://soundcloud.com/richard_uttley/sets/will-eaves-the-point-of-distraction]

4.

Olivier Messiaen (1908–92): *Catalogue d'Oiseaux*, 1956–58; *Petites esquisses d'Oiseaux*, 1984
Paul Kim, piano. *Olivier Messiaen: Complete Works for Piano, Vol. 1*. Centaur CRC2567-69, 2001

Modest Mussorgsky (1839–81): *Pictures at an Exhibition*, 1874
Mikhail Pletnev, piano. *Mussorgsky and Tchaikovsky: Works for piano*. Erato 482 0552, 1989/2005
Carlo Maria Giulini, conducting the Chicago Symphony Orchestra; orch. Maurice Ravel. *Mussorgsky: Pictures at an Exhibition*. DG 2530 783, 1976

Leonard Bernstein (1918–90): *West Side Story*, 1957
Leonard Bernstein. *West Side Story* (Original Cast Recording). Columbia SK60724, 1957/1998

Anon: 'The Last Post' (bugle call), c.1790s
Jamie Smith, Grimethorpe Colliery Band. 2022. https://www.youtube.com/watch?v=onKaOa6dQCs

Kate Bush (1958–): 'Kite' (from *The Kick Inside*, 1978)
Kate Bush, vocal. *The Kick Inside*. EMI EMC 3223, 1978

Prince: 'Tamborine' (from *Around the World in a Day*, 1985)
Prince and the Revolution. *Around the World in a Day*. Paisley Park 925 286-1, 1985

John Cage (1912–92): '4'33"', 1952
Frank Zappa et al. *A Chance Operation – The John Cage Tribute*. Koch International Classics 3 7238 2, 1993

Wolfgang Amadeus Mozart (1756–91): Piano Sonata in A Minor. K310, 1778
Mitsuko Uchida, piano. *Mozart: The Piano Sonatas*. Phillips 422 115/6/7-2, 1988

Béla Bartók (1881–1945): Six Dances in Bulgarian Rhythm (V) (from *Mikrokosmos* Book VI, 1926–39)
Gyôrgy Sandór, piano. *Bartók: Mikrokosmos*. MP2K 52528, 1961/1993

Will Eaves: Two Birds from *Four Diptychs*, 2022
Richard Uttley, piano. [https://soundcloud.com/richard_uttley/sets/will-eaves-the-point-of-distraction]

5.

Carla Bley (1936–2023): 'Real Life Hits'; 'The Lord is Listening To Ya, Hallelujah', 1981
The Carla Bley Band. *Carla Bley: Live!*. WATT/ECM 2313 112, 1982

Erik Satie (1866–1925): Trois Gymnopédies, 1888; Trois Gnossiennes, c.1890; *Pièces Froides*, 1897
Jean-Yves Thibaudet, piano. *Satie: The complete solo piano music*. Decca 473 620-2, 2003

Charles Mingus (1922–79): 'Group Dancers' (from *The Black Saint and the Sinner Lady*, 1963)
Charles Mingus, bass and piano, et al. *The Black Saint and the Sinner Lady*. Impulse! AS-35, 1963

Johann Sebastian Bach: Toccatas BWV 910-916, c1704–1710
Angela Hewitt, piano. *Bach: The Toccatas*. Hyperion CDA67310, 2002

Johann Sebastian Bach: Toccata and Fugue in D Minor BWV 565, c1703–1707
Marie-Claire Alain, organ. *Bach: Complete Works for Organ*. Erato 2292 45732 2, 1980

Franz Schubert (1797–1828): Impromptu No. 2 in E Flat Major, Op. 90 D899, 1827
Mitsuko Uchida, piano. *Mitsuko Uchida Plays Schubert*. Phillips 4756 282, 2004

Ludwig Van Beethoven (1770–1827): Piano Sonata No. 7 in D Major, Op. 10, No. 3, 1798
Martha Argerich, piano. *Early Recordings*. DG 479 6065, 1960/2016

Will Eaves: Two Idioms from *Four Diptychs*, 2022
Richard Uttley, piano. [https://soundcloud.com/richard_uttley/sets/will-eaves-the-point-of-distraction]

6.

William Byrd (1539/40–1623): 'Pavana: The Earl of Salisbury' (from *Parthenia*, 1611)
Davitt Moroney, muselar virginal. *William Byrd: Complete Keyboard Music*. Hyperion CDS44461/7, 1999

Orlando Gibbons (1583–1625): 'The Lord of Salisbury, his Pavin' (from *Parthenia*, 1611)
Christopher Hogwood, harpsichord. *Orlando Gibbons: Keyboard Music*. L'Oiseau-Lyre DSLO 515, 1975

John Dowland: 'Lachrimae Pavan', 1596
Paul O'Dette, lute. *John Dowland: Complete Lute Works, Vol 2*. Harmonia Mundi 907161, 1996

Maurice Ravel (1875–1937): 'Pavane pour une infante défunte', 1899
Vladimir Ashkenazy, piano. *Ravel: Gaspard de la nuit, Pavane & Valses Nobles et Sentimentales*. Decca 410 2551

George Gershwin (1898–1937): 'Fascinating Rhythm' (from *Lady, Be Good!*, 1924)

Tony Bennett, vocal. *Tony Bennett at Carnegie Hall*. Columbia C2S 823, 1962

Thelonius Monk (1917–82): 'North of the Sunset' and 'Ask Me Now', 1965

Thelonius Monk, piano. *Solo Monk*. Columbia CL2349, 1965

Franz Liszt (1811–86): 'Trübe Wolken (Nuages Gris)', 1881

Alfred Brendel, piano. *Liszt: Sonata in B Minor, Funérailles and other works*. Phillips 434 078-2, 1992

Will Eaves: 'Pavan', 2022

Richard Uttley, piano. [https://soundcloud.com/richard_uttley/sets/will-eaves-the-point-of-distraction]

7.

Ben Watt (1962–) and Tracey Thorn (1962–): 'Driving' (from *The Language of Life*, 1990)

Everything But the Girl. *The Language of Life*. Atlantic 82057-2, 1990

Johann Sebastian Bach: Minuet in D Minor, BWV Anh 132 (from *Notebook for Anna Magdalena Bach*, 1725)

Mahan Esfahani, harpsichord and clavichord; Carolyn Sampson, soprano. *Notebooks for Anna Magdalena Bach*. Hyperion CDA68387, 2023; Giovanni Mazzocchin, piano. *J. S. Bach: Notebook for Anna Magdalena Bach* (1725). OnClassical OC21108B, 2021

Acknowledgements

I am grateful to Merton College, Oxford, for a Visiting Research Fellowship that supported the composition of *The Point of Distraction* and its accompanying music.

I would also like to thank Andrew Frampton, Zoë Martlew, Christopher Austin, Sophie Scott and Susanna Eastburn for their friendly interest in this project; Luciano Williamson for engraving the scores; Richard Uttley for playing them so beautifully; and my teachers: Barbara Shergold, Peter Jezard, Mary King and Kevin Duggan.